For Julian.
For José.
For my friend and compadre David, you are missed.
For fathers and sons, papás y hijos.

ABOUT THIS BOOK

The illustrations in this book were done in oils over acrylics on Strathmore 500 illustration board. This book was edited by Esther Cajahuaringa and designed by Véronique Lefèvre Sweet and Christine Kettner. The production was supervised by Patricia Alvarado, and the production editor was Marisa Finkelstein. The text was set in Love Ya Like a Sister Solid, and the display type is Wolfpack Regular.

Rafa Counts on Papá

By Joe Cepeda

LB

LITTLE, BROWN AND COMPANY
New York   Boston

Rafa is the happiest when he knows
exactly how much.

And his papá is too.

They know exactly how long Rafa's train is.

They know exactly how far they can
run in twenty-two minutes.

Rafa and his papá even measure just how
high their dog, Euclid, can jump.

They climb exactly fourteen branches
before they get to their favorite one.
"There's nothing we can't measure, right, Dad?
Measuring is what we do best!" says Rafa.

"Let's measure which cloud is the puffiest!"

"Which is the yellowest?
Which is the bounciest?

...the fluffiest?
Or who is the fanciest?!"

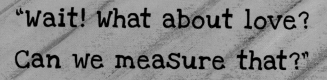

"Wait! What about love?
Can we measure that?"

"Is love as tall and scrumptious as this?!"

"Or is love as long and floaty as this?!"

"And what about me?
How much do you love me?"

"IS your love for me as tall as Tío Humberto?

As mighty as an ox?

As sturdy as an oak tree?

As perfect as pancakes?
As steady as a Swiss watch?
Or as deep as the Grand Canyon?!"

"How much?!"

"This much."

And THAT MUCH is
just fine with Rafa.